# 32

# Short

# Uplifting

# Stories

A collection of motivational, moral and inspirational short stories.

Written by **Christopher Starr**

Published by **Story Wisdom**

# 32 Short Uplifting Stories.

## by Christopher Starr

**First Edition**

# Table of Contents

# A Day at The Theme Park

A woman and her young daughter visit a local theme park.

They stand in line for the Thunderbolt, the park's biggest roller coaster.

"Almost there," she says with a tired smile.

The little girl stomps her foot.

"This is taking forever!" she shouts. "I want to ride now!"

People hear the commotion and begin to stare.

The woman kneels to the girl's level.

"Sarah," she whispers, "be patient and calm down."

The girl stops screaming.

After the ride, they head to a snack stand. The line is long, and the smell of popcorn makes their stomachs growl.

The girl grows hungry and impatient.

"I'm starving!" she whines, grabbing a bag of chips from the stand and ripping it open.

"Hey!" the cashier calls out.

The woman quickly pays for the chips and turns to the girl with a stern look.

"Sarah, calm down and be patient."

As they walk through the park, the girl's eyes widen at the colourful balloons for sale.

"I want one!" she demands, reaching for a red balloon.

The woman catches her hand.

"Not today," she says. "We've already spent our budget."

The girl's face turns red, and she throws herself on the ground, kicking and screaming.

People stop to watch. Some shake their heads, while others whisper and point.

The woman wants to explode but takes a deep breath instead. She kneels down again.

"Sarah, just calm down and be patient."

After a while, the girl stops crying.

"There we go. Let's enjoy the rest of our day, okay?"

Hand in hand, they walk toward the exit.

Suddenly, a lady approaches them.

"Excuse me," the lady says. "I hope you don't mind, but I've been watching you today."

The woman tenses, fearing the worst.

"I just wanted to say you dealt with your daughter Sarah well. Your patience is admirable," the lady says, smiling.

The woman smiles back and lets out a small laugh.

"Thank you," she says.

"But Sarah isn't my daughter."

"That's my name."

# The Beauty Within

Olivia stares at her phone, her heart racing.

*Ping!* A new message from Alex, a guy she's been talking to on a dating app.

They've been chatting for weeks, sharing jokes and dreams.

But Alex has never seen Olivia. She's done everything she can to avoid it.

Her fingers graze the large, bumpy growth on her cheek.

The mirror reflects a face she despises.

"How could anyone like me?" she mutters miserably.

Alex's message pops up. "Want to meet for coffee tomorrow?"

Olivia's stomach drops.

She types back quickly. "I'm sorry, I can't."

"Why not?" Alex replies.

Her fingers tremble as she writes:

" You won't like me when you see me."

There's no reply.

Olivia's heart sinks. She's sure she's scared him away.

Then, another message appears.

"Nonsense! Plus, I should have told you earlier. I'm blind. So, whatever you look like doesn't matter to me. I like you for who you are inside."

Olivia breathes a sigh of relief.

Feeling reassured, she agrees to meet.

The next day, they meet at a small café nearby. Olivia's hands tremble as she steps inside.

She spots a man with dark glasses and a cane sitting at a corner table.

"Alex?" she asks softly.

He turns toward her voice and smiles.

"Olivia! I'm so glad you came!" He exclaims.

As they talk, Olivia forgets about her growth.

Alex listens, laughs at her jokes, and makes her feel special.

For the first time in years, she feels beautiful.

Weeks turn into months. Olivia and Alex spend more and more time together.

But Olivia worries.

Should she tell Alex the truth about her growth?

What if he feels it when they hug or hold hands?

One day, as they walk in the park, she decides to be brave.

"Alex," she whispers, her voice shaking. "I need to tell you something about my face."

Before she can continue, Alex squeezes her hand.

"Olivia, I love you. All of you. Nothing about your face will change that."

Olivia's eyes fill with tears. She hugs Alex tightly, feeling truly accepted for the first time in her life.

Two years pass. Olivia and Alex get married.

They're happier than they ever thought possible.

But Olivia falls ill.

Doctors say her growth has turned into a dangerous tumour.

Despite their best efforts, Olivia grows weaker each day.

Eventually, she passes away.

At Olivia's funeral, people gather to say goodbye.

As the crowd begins to leave, a woman notices Alex walking away.

He moves confidently, without his cane.

"Excuse me, sir," the woman calls out.

"I know you're blind. Do you need any help?" she shouts.

Alex turns and shakes his head.

"That's okay, friend." He replies and continues to walk.

She frowns. "But how can you see where you are going?"

"Oh I'm not blind" he shouts back.

The woman jaw drops.

"What do you mean?! Why pretend?!" She exclaims.

He smiles.

"Oh, I only said that for her."

"So, she would reveal her real beauty."

"Her true self."

# The New Neighbour

Sarah's hands shake as she unlocks her new front door.

The house is small and needs paint. It is nothing like her old mansion.

"I can do this," she whispers to herself, her voice trembling.

Her phone buzzes.

A text from her old friend Jenna pops up. "Watch out! Poor people always want handouts!"

Sarah shrugs it off, determined to make a new start.

The next morning, there is a knock at the door.

She opens it to find a woman holding a baby.

"Hi! I'm Lisa from next door," the woman says with a big smile. "Can I borrow some eggs? I'm making pancakes."

Sarah remembers Jenna's warning, but Lisa's friendly face makes her want to help.

"Okay," she agrees.

She retrieves the eggs and hands them to Lisa.

"You're the best!" Lisa grins.

"Welcome to the neighbourhood!"

Sarah closes the door and carries on with her day.

Over the next few days, she unpacks her boxes and sets up her new home office, beginning to work on her design business again.

But every time she looks out the window, neighbours either look away or hurry past. She feels like an outsider.

On the third day, Sarah hears yet another knock.

This time, an old man with a cane stands at her door.

"Hello, I'm Tom," he mumbles in a shaky voice. "Could I borrow some butter? My hands hurt too much to go to the store today."

Sarah wants to say no, but Tom looks exhausted.

"Just a second," she mutters.

She reluctantly retrieves the butter and gives it to him.

Tom smiles. "Thank you, dear. It's nice to see a new face around here."

Sarah forces a smile back.

Two people asking for things in three days? Maybe Jenna was right after all.

The next day, Sarah is on an important work call when someone knocks again.

Annoyed, she stomps to the door and yanks it open.

A teenage girl stands there, twisting her hair, shuffling from foot to foot.

"Hi, I'm Amy from down the street," the girl says. "I want to bake something for my mom. She's been down lately. But I'm out of flour. Could I borrow some?"

Sarah face turns red. Anger begins to bubble within her, but Amy looks worried.

Burying her anger yet again, she decides to help the young girl.

"Wait here." She storms off to grab the flour, then thrusts it into Amy's hands.

"This is the last time!" Sarah growls.

Amy's face lights up. "Thank you so much! This means a lot."

Sarah slams the door shut.

That night, Sarah sits among her unpacked boxes, feeling more alone than ever.

"Enough," she declares out loud. "I'm done being nice. I need to protect what I have left."

She hatches a plan to avoid her neighbours. No more lending things. No more being friendly. It isn't nice, but she must look out for herself.

The next morning, Sarah decides to go for a walk. She opens her door, ready to ignore everyone. But something surprises her.

As she steps outside, she spots a small box on her doorstep.

Intrigued, she decides to open it.

Inside sits a beautiful cake, still warm.

She quirks an eyebrow, glancing up the empty street.

She decides to investigate it further and finds a note:

Dear New Neighbour,

We know moving is hard. We don't have a lot, but we wanted to give you something. So, we all came together to make this cake for you.

Welcome to the neighbourhood!

# The Boy Outside the Shop

Another day, another dollar for Mr. Grump.

He sighs as he flips the "Open" for what seems like a millionth time.

His grocery store, which he has owned for almost all his life, is often targeted by kids.

They play outside, making lots of noise and putting customers off.

One day, he spots a small boy sitting on the sidewalk in front of his shop.

Hey, kid!" Mr. Grump barks.

"Go sit somewhere else. You're bad for business." He shouts, waving his fist.

But the little boy remains seated.

Mr. Grump growls, then goes back inside.

He tries to ignore the boy but can't help stealing glances at him through the window.

Hours pass, yet the boy still sits there.

Mr. Grump notices the boy's stomach growling.

"If I feed him, maybe he'll leave," he thinks.

He grabs a sandwich and a juice box, then marches outside.

"Here." He thrusts the food at the boy. "Now scram."

The boy devours the food quickly, but remains seated, not moving an inch.

As evening comes, Mr. Grump spots the boy shivering.

With a sigh, he pulls out a warm jacket and a blanket from the store's winter section.

"Take these," he insists. "But then you got to go home, okay?"

The boy wraps himself in the blanket but again stays put.

Mr. Grump throws his hands up in frustration.

How on earth can he get him to leave? He could chase the boy away. He could ignore him. He could call the police.

Then, a thought strikes him like lightning.

Maybe the kid just wants someone to talk to. Mr. Grump takes a deep breath and sits down beside him on the sidewalk.

"So," he says awkwardly, "what's your name?"

The boy raises his head.

"My names Tommy." He states, with a smile.

The two continue to talk for a little while.

As they talk, Mr. Grump feels something strange - he is enjoying the boy's company.

He suddenly narrows his gaze.

"I have a question. Why do you sit here every day?" Mr. Grump asks.

Tommy bows his head. "My mom told me that if anything ever bad happened to her, then I am to visit here."

"She passed away a few weeks ago, so I am just doing what she told me." He sobs.

Mr. Grump's brow furrows. "Sorry to hear about your mom. But why here? There are so many other shops or charities you could go to?"

The boy pauses, looking up at Mr. Grump.

"My dad owns the shop."

# The Seed of Leadership

Mr. Chen, the CEO of Integrity Industries, paces in his office.

The company needs a new leader, someone who truly understands their values. He needs to find the right person but doesn't know how.

Suddenly an idea strikes him.

He calls in his top three candidates: Alex, Bianca, and Carlos.

"I have a special task for you," Mr. Chen announces.

He hands each of them a small pot and a seed.

"Grow these seeds. In three months, whoever has the biggest plant will become the new CEO!" He announces.

The candidates leave, excited at the challenge ahead.

For three months, Alex, Bianca, and Carlos tend to their seeds.

They water, fertilize, and talk to their plants every day.

Each dreams of the day they'll present their thriving plant to Mr. Chen.

The day of revelation finally arrives.

Alex and Bianca stride in confidently, carrying lush, green plants that nearly burst from their pots.

Carlos shuffles in last, head down, carrying only an empty pot.

Mr. Chen raises an eyebrow. "Carlos, what happened to your plant?"

Carlos takes a deep breath. "I'm sorry, sir," he says. "I tried everything but couldn't make it grow."

The room falls silent. Then Mr. Chen breaks into a wide smile.

"Congratulations, Carlos," he declares. "You're the new CEO of Integrity Industries."

Alex and Bianca gasp.

"But he didn't grow anything! That's not fair!" They protest. Unable to understand how their hard work and success have been overshadowed by Carlos's honesty.

Mr. Chen holds up his hand.

"At this company, we pride ourselves on honesty and integrity above all else. Isn't that, right?" He asks.

Alex and Bianca shrug, before returning a small nod.

"So, tell me," Mr. Chen continues, his voice growing stern, "how did you both manage to grow such impressive plants when all the seeds I gave you were fake?"

# A Heart Full of Love

Two sisters, Lily and Rose, live in a small house on the edge of town. They have no parents, only each other, which is enough for them.

Lily, the older sister, possesses strength and health.

Rose, the younger sister, often falls ill and spends much time in bed.

One day, as Lily reads Rose a story.

"I wish I could be strong like you," she sighs.

Lily squeezes her hand.

"You're strong in your own way, Rosie."

But Rose's eyes sadden. "I want to run and play like other kids." She whimpers.

That night, Lily wishes upon the brightest star she can see. "Please," she whispers, "let Rose be healthy and strong."

The following day, Rose wakes up feeling worse than ever.

She struggles to breathe.

"Hospital," Lily says, already dialling for help. "We need to get you to the hospital."

At the hospital, doctors rush around Rose's bed.

There is a problem with her heart.

Lily clutches Rose's hand. "Don't worry," she says, forcing a smile. "After this, you'll be strong like me. I promise."

The doctors speak with Rose before heading to the operating room.

Hours pass until eventually the operation is complete.

Rose wakes up feeling strange. Her chest doesn't hurt anymore. She feels strong. Excited, she jumps out of bed.

"I need to tell Lily!" she shouts.

She makes her way down the hallway, looking for her sister.

A nurse stops her in the hallway. "Whoa there, where are you going so fast?!" She exclaims.

Rose bounces on her toes. "To find my sister! She was right—I do feel stronger now!"

The nurse's smile fades.

"Oh, sweetie," she whispers. "I am sorry."

Rose frowns. "Sorry? Why? I feel great!" She remarks.

The nurse places a gentle hand on Rose's shoulder, her eyes watery.

"Your heart was too weak to keep going"

"So, your sister gave you hers."

# The Most Precious Hour

Mr. Thompson never stops working, labouring from sunrise to sunset.

He is always busy, always tired.

At home, his daughter Lily watches the clock, waiting for her dad to return.

One evening, as Mr. Thompson gulps his coffee, Lily tugs on his sleeve.

"Dad," she whispers, "how much do you earn per hour?"

Mr. Thompson frowns. "Why do you want to know?"

Lily shuffles her feet. "I want to buy something."

Mr. Thompson sighs. "I earn $10 an hour, sweetie. How much is the thing you want to buy?"

"$10," she replies quietly.

Mr. Thompson frowns, running a hand through his hair.

"Look, Lily, I'm sorry, but I can't give you that much. I can give you half - it's all I can afford. Just don't waste it. I work hard for that money."

Lily takes the money, feeling a little annoyed that it isn't enough.

Later that night, Mr. Thompson overhears Lily talking to her mom.

"Mom, can I have $5?" Lily asks.

Mrs. Thompson hesitates, then agrees. "What's it for, honey?"

"I want to buy something special," Lily explains.

Mr. Thompson, listening from the other room, feels his anger rising.

He'd told Lily they couldn't afford extras, yet here she is, asking for more!

Unable to let it go, he storms into Lily's room.

"What do you think you're doing?" he shouts.

"I told you we didn't have much money, and you still asked your mom for more!"

Lily begins to shake, tears welling in her eyes.

"But $5 wasn't enough," she trembles.

"Enough for what?" Mr. Thompson demands.

"What is so special that you need $10 for?"

Lily holds out the $10 with trembling hands.

Her voice is barely a whisper.

"An hour of your time."

# A Meal of Kindness

Mr. Gray walks down Main Street.

"Yuck, look at that!" onlookers shout.

"His grubby appearance is spoiling the area!"

He doesn't have a penny to his name.

His stomach growls: he hasn't eaten in days.

As Mr. Gray walks past a restaurant, he notices a half-eaten sandwich on an empty table.

He enters the restaurant, glances around nervously, then reaches for it.

"Hey!" someone shouts. "Get away from there!"

Mr. Gray jumps back, embarrassed, but he has to eat.

Hunger drives him to the next table. He manages to grab a cold French fry before someone throws a napkin at him.

"Go away!" they yell. "You don't belong here!"

Shame burns Mr. Gray's cheeks, but he is starving. At the last table, he finds a plate with half a burger and some fries. He reaches for it.

Suddenly, two boys appear. "Hey, what are you doing?" they groan. "That's our food."

Mr. Gray freezes, fearing what might happen next. The boys exchange mischievous glances, then look back at Mr. Gray.

"Wait here," they say, and both hurry away.

Mr. Gray considers running, but he knows they could catch him.

Minutes pass, and his anxiety grows. Just as he decides to make a run for it, the boys reappear.

They carry a tray piled high with steaming hot food - a big burger, crispy fries, and a cool, large soda.

"Here," the taller boy says, holding out the tray. "This is for you, sir."

Mr Gray frowns. "For... me?"

The shorter boy nods.

"We're sorry about before. We couldn't watch you eat leftovers."

"So we got you your own proper meal," the taller boy adds, "to eat all for yourself."

# Overlooked Blessings

Jake lies in bed late at night, dreaming of a better life.

He wants money, fame, and love.

That night, Jake decides to pray.

"I want to be rich when I grow up," he whispers. "I want people to notice and respect me. I want to find the love of my life. Please help this happen, God."

He drifts off to sleep.

The next morning, Jake sets off and makes his way to the convenience store. Suddenly, he hears a noise.

"Excuse me, young man," an old man calls. "Could you help me for a moment?"

Jake hesitates. He is in a hurry to get to the store before it closes. "Sorry," he mumbles. "I'm in a rush."

At the store, Jake buys his favourite candy bar. As he turns to leave, the girl at the checkout calls out, "Wait! You forgot your receipt!"

"It's okay. You keep it," Jake replies.

On his way home, he notices a reporter recording an interview. They ask if Jake would like to be a part of it.

"Sorry, I need to get back in time for my favourite TV show," he states. "I'm already late."

Later that night, lying in bed, Jake feels annoyed at God.

"Why didn't you give me what I asked for?" he demands.

But God doesn't speak.

As Jake drifts off to sleep, he finds himself in a strange, misty place. He hears a voice.

"Jake, I heard you complaining that I did not give you what you wished for. But I did."

Jake frowns. "What do you mean? You didn't give me anything." He growls.

The voice chuckles softly.

"You wished to be rich. The old man in the park that you refused to help? He was the CEO of a huge company looking for his next apprentice."

"You wished for love. Remember the girl at the store? She wrote her phone number on your receipt, the one that you didn't take."

"You wanted fame. That interview? The one you skipped because you couldn't wait to get home? That ended up being broadcast to over 500 million people worldwide."

"I... I didn't know," Jake stutters.

"I gave you opportunities," the voice says gently.

"You just never took them."

# The Time That Matters Most

Mr. Parker is a workaholic.

He works two jobs to give his son, Tommy, a good life, but it means he rarely sees the boy.

When he does, he is always tired and exhausted.

One day, after a long shift, he returns home and is shocked.

Spread across the entire living room floor are his prized watch collection, all battered and broken.

From the corner of his eye, he spots Tommy hitting one with a toy hammer.

"What is going on? What have you done, Tommy?" Mr. Parker exclaims. "This is my prized collection!"

Tommy begins to speak, but Mr. Parker is too angry to listen. "Get to your room now; I don't want to hear it," he shouts furiously waving his fists in the air.

The next day, Mr. Parker calms down and decides to approach Tommy to find out why he did what he did.

"Tommy, you know Daddy works really hard, and you know those watches meant a lot to me," he whispers. "So why break them all?"

Tommy's eyes fill with tears.

"I'm sorry, Daddy, but I was only making you a gift."

"A gift?" Mr. Parker raises an eyebrow. "Well, where is it?"

Tommy runs to his room and returns with a box. "It's in here," he states.

Mr. Parker opens the box to find a clock made from all the pieces of his watches. He furrows his brow in confusion.

"I don't understand, Tommy. Why have you built me a clock?"

Tommy raises his chin and narrows his gaze.

"Well, I know you work so hard. So I built it so you will always know when it's time to come home and play with me."

# The Best Revenge

Jack is a shy boy, obsessed with Sarah, a girl in his class.

She is perfect - pretty, popular, and rich. A far cry from Jack's life.

Jack watches her every day in awe, dreaming of a future with her. One day, after many months, he finally works up the courage to ask her on a date.

Jack's heart races as he approaches. "Hey Sarah, I was just wondering, would you like to go on a date with me, maybe to the cinema?"

Time stands still. The hallway falls silent. Sarah stares at him for a second, then bursts out laughing. "Me with you? No chance. I don't date charity cases."

Jack's face reddens. His heart sinks. The hallway erupts in laughter. He runs to the bathroom, staring at himself in the mirror. "I'll show them. I'm going to become someone," Jack declares. "No one will laugh at me again."

Over the next few years, Jack studies relentlessly.

He works multiple part-time jobs and saves up a lot of money.

After college, he uses the money he's earned to open his own tech company, working tirelessly day and night to make it a success.

Fifteen years later, he has succeeded. He is now the CEO of a multimillion-dollar company.

Jack sits in his office, admiring his achievement, when a job application from a candidate he is meeting today catches his eye. It's a name he knows well: Sarah Johnson.

Suddenly, emotions from that day come flooding back - embarrassment, shame, rejection.

But before he has a chance to dwell on them, his receptionist opens the door.

"Jack, Sarah is here for the interview."

"Oh, okay, send her in," Jack stutters.

Sarah walks into the office, not recognizing the man before her.

Jack could have sent her away or revealed who he is, but instead, he smiles and conducts the interview professionally.

"Welcome aboard," he says at the end, extending his hand.

Sarah's face lights up with relief and gratitude; she has been out of work for months.

Months pass, and Sarah thrives in her new job, quickly rising to a management position.

Then comes the night of the annual work party. Sarah finally realizes who Jack is.

Embarrassed, she approaches him to apologize. "Jack, I'm so sorry. I didn't recognize you. You've changed so much from school."

"That's okay," Jack replies with a smile.

"I'm so sorry for the way I treated you back then. I guess you want to fire me now?" Sarah concedes.

Jack raises an eyebrow. "Why?"

"For what I did to you in school," she states.

Jack smiles. "What you did to me in school motivated me to become the man I am today."

She frowns. "You're not angry? Don't you want revenge after how I treated you?"

"Of course not," Jack assures her.

"The best revenge was becoming someone I'm proud of. If anything, I should be thanking you."

# The Promise Bench

No matter the weather, come rain or shine, an old man visits the park and sits on the same bench every day, always alone.

One crisp winter day, a curious young boy named Max spots the man.

Intrigued by why he always sits there, Max approaches him.

"Excuse me, sir, why do you always sit here?" Max inquires.

The old man smiles. "I'm waiting for somebody special."

The boy nods and carries on his day.

Weeks pass, and Max continues to see the same man on the bench every day. Unable to contain his curiosity any longer, Max approaches the bench again.

"Is your special someone coming soon?" he asks.

The old man chuckles softly. "I hope so, my boy. I hope so."

As months go by, Max grows more and more intrigued. No matter the weather, the man still sits there. Max's concern grows with each passing day, beginning to wonder if the man is sick.

Finally, on a sunny June afternoon, Max decides to approach the man again, but this time with a different question - a question that has been nagging at him for months.

He cautiously approaches the old man.

"Hi sir, I hope you don't mind, but we spoke before, months ago," Max begins.

"Oh yes, I remember you," the man replies cheerfully.

"Well, I remember you told me you were waiting for somebody," Max continues, "but I have seen you sitting here alone every day for nearly an entire year. I don't think they are coming."

The man bursts out laughing. "You're right; they probably won't."

Max frowns. "I don't understand. Who exactly are you waiting for?"

The old man's eyes mist over as he whispers, "My wife."

Max's eyes widen in surprise. "Your wife? But it's been so long!" he exclaims. "Where is she?"

The old man's weathered face breaks into a tender smile. He pats the empty bench beside him gently.

"Oh, she's right here," he states with a smile.

Max frowns once more, raising an eyebrow. "But sir, there's no one there."

"Oh, I know. Don't worry, boy, I'm not crazy," the old man assures him. "This is where we first met 60 years ago. We were young, like you. We fell in love right here on this bench."

He gazes wistfully into the distance. "You see, I'm not waiting for her to come. I'm just keeping our promise to meet here, no matter what."

# The Troublesome Child

It is the first day of her new job. Ms. Thompson is on her way to begin her journey at a new school.

Although nervous, she is excited at the chance to change children's lives through the power of learning.

Upon entering the school, she is ushered to the teachers' lounge for a debrief from the other teachers.

"Watch out for a kid in your class - Rick," one of the teachers shouts. "He's one of the biggest troublemakers in the school."

"He's going to make your life miserable," another one adds.

Ms. Thompson is a little nervous, but she has always believed that any student can have potential, no matter how they behave.

With that in mind, her first class begins.

She enters the room and immediately sees the boy they were talking about - messy hair, feet on the desk, eating a candy bar.

"Rick Stevens, I assume?" she asks.

"Who's it to you?" he snaps.

"I'm your new teacher. Could you please sit nicely and stop eating?" she requests.

"Could you stop being such a dumb teacher?" he growls.

Ms. Thompson holds her nerve and smiles at him before calmly starting the lesson.

Throughout the entire lesson, the boy shouts rude comments, disrupting the lesson at any opportunity he gets.

But instead of scolding him or sending him to the principal's office, she stays calm, continuing the lesson and pretending not to notice.

When the bell rings, Ms. Thompson calls out, "Rick, could you stay for a moment?"

Rick's scowl deepens. "You must hate me already," he mutters.

Ms. Thompson smiles gently. "No, Rick. I think you're very smart."

Rick's eyes widen in surprise.

Ms. Thompson reaches into her bag and pulls out a thick book. She could have lectured Rick or punished him. Instead, she holds out the book.

"Could you please read this by tomorrow?" she asks.

Rick stares at the book, then at Ms. Thompson. "Wait, you're not making me stay or giving me detention? All I have to do is read this book?"

"Yep," Ms. Thompson replies.

"Erm Okay," Rick agrees, slightly confused.

The next day, Rick returns the book. "I finished it," he states.

"Excellent," Ms. Thompson replies. "What did you think about it?"

To her delight, Rick launches into a detailed analysis of the book, showcasing a wealth of knowledge.

This pattern continues for weeks. Each day, Ms. Thompson gives Rick a new, more challenging book. Each day, Rick returns with thoughtful insights.

As the school year nears its end, Rick's transformation is remarkable. His grades have soared, and he actively participates in class discussions.

After the final bell on the last day, Rick approaches Ms. Thompson's desk.

"Why did you believe in me when everyone else thought I was trouble?" he asks.

Ms. Thompson smiles. "Do you remember that first book I gave you?"

Rick nods.

"It was a university-level text on advanced physics," she reveals. "You understood it perfectly."

Rick's jaw drops. "But... but why didn't you tell me?"

Ms. Thompson leans forward.

"Because you needed to discover your potential, Rick. You were never trouble. You were just bored."

# The Apple of Kindness

Mr. Goldstein loves to work. It is all he knows. But his son, Alex, is the opposite.

Mr. Goldstein often becomes frustrated that Alex can't be more like himself.

At dinner that night, Mr. Goldstein's frustration boils over. "You need to learn the value of hard work," he tells Alex.

"I was making millions at your age, yet you do nothing every day."

Alex shrugs.

Suddenly, an idea strikes Mr. Goldstein. "I know just the thing to teach you a lesson. Meet me at 7 a.m. tomorrow."

The next morning arrives, and Alex meets his dad. Mr. Goldstein presents Alex with a large box of shiny red apples.

"Sell these in the town square," he instructs. "Then you'll understand the value of money and hard work."

Alex looks at the box, nods, and sets off.

In the bustling town square, he sets up his apple stand. As he arranges his fruit store, he notices a scruffy homeless man sharing a small loaf of bread with others nearby.

Alex continues to watch the man for hours. Every time someone gives something to the homeless man, he immediately shares it with others.

Alex feels inspired.

That evening, Mr. Goldstein eagerly awaits his son's return.

When Alex walks in empty-handed, Mr. Goldstein's eyes light up. "Where are all the apples?" he asks, excited. "Did you sell them already? I'm so proud, son."

Alex takes a deep breath. "No, Dad. I didn't sell them."

Mr. Goldstein's smile fades. "Well, where are they?" he demands.

"I gave them away," Alex whispers.

Mr. Goldstein's face turns red. "Gave them away? Why on earth would you do that?" he shouts.

Alex looks his father in the eye. "I gave them to people in need."

His dad frowns. "What do you mean?"

Alex smiles. "Dad, you wanted to teach me the value of money, and I appreciate that. But those people in the square - they taught me the value of kindness."

# Old Friends

Frank and John are two best friends who have known each other since school.

Every week for 50 years, they meet in the local park to play their favourite game: chess.

No matter the weather - rain, shine, snow, or hail - nothing stops them.

However, one day, on a cold, frosty morning, John is late for the first time.

Frank waits and waits, but John never shows up.

This happens the next day and the day after that.

After many days, a woman approaches Frank. "Hi, are you Frank?" she asks.

"I certainly am, and who might you be?" he replies.

"I'm John's daughter," she says. "I'm sorry to inform you, but John wasn't feeling too well. He passed away in his sleep a few days ago."

Frank's heart sinks.

"I'm really sorry; I know you two were close," the woman continues. "I just wanted to save you the bother of coming here every day to wait for him."

"Okay, thanks for letting me know," a teary-eyed Frank replies.

The woman leaves, and Frank sits there in silence, unmoving.

For the next few weeks, Frank still turns up at the park, equipped with his chessboard every time.

Onlookers think he's crazy, that he's lost his mind, but Frank doesn't care.

One day, like clockwork, Frank arrives at the park and sets up his chessboard, even though he has no one to play with.

It is then that a young boy, no older than 10 years old, approaches him.

"Hi sir, do you mind if I sit down and play with you?" the boy inquires.

"Of course," Frank replies, feeling that he has met the boy before.

"I'm sorry, I don't really know how to play. Can you teach me?"

"No problem," Frank says. "I hope you don't mind, but you look really familiar. I feel as though I've seen those eyes before. Have we met?"

The boy shakes his head. "No, you have never met me, but I have heard a lot about you."

Suddenly, it clicks. Frank's eyes widen.

"Your grandfather sent you, didn't he?"

The boy nods, a small smile on his face.

"He said you'd be waiting."

# The Lesson of a Lifetime

Mark's hand trembles as he holds his college acceptance letter. He's been accepted to a prestigious teaching program.

His dream has come true. He rushes to tell his father, longing to make him proud.

"I made it, Dad," Mark exclaims. "I got accepted into the teacher program."

But his dad scowls. "A teacher? Get a real job," Mr. Johnson scoffs. "Teaching won't make you rich, son. You need a business job, like me."

Despite his father's disapproval, Mark stands his ground. "It's not about being rich, Dad. It's about making a difference."

Mr. Johnson berates his son. "You're making a huge mistake. If you want to ruin your life, that's on you. But I want no part of it." He shouts.

From that day forward, their relationship deteriorates.

Years pass, and Mark throws himself into his teaching career, pouring his heart and soul into every lesson. He rarely speaks to his father.

Weeks grow into months, and months into years. Then, one autumn evening, Mark's phone rings.

His mother's voice trembles on the other end. "Your father's in the hospital. It's serious."

Mark rushes to the hospital immediately.

Upon his arrival, he finds his father pale and weak, hooked up to multiple machines.

The doctor's words are grim. Mr. Johnson needs expensive treatment they just can't afford.

Mark sits by his father's bed, feeling helpless. His salary is not nearly enough to pay for the treatment needed.

The next day, Mark returns to work, and his students catch wind of what has happened.

Later that night, Mark receives another phone call. "You need to come to the hospital now. Something strange is happening." She insists.

He arrives at the hospital

He almost falls over with the sight in front of him.

A long line as far as the eye can see leading to his father's hospital room - all his students, past and present.

They have brought cards, flowers, and most importantly, donations.

"We heard about your dad, Mr. Mark," one whispers. "So we wanted to help."

Mr. Johnson watches in bewilderment. "Who are all these people?" he whimpers.

Mark smiles. "They're my students, Dad."

Mr. Johnson frowns. "But I don't understand. I'm a stranger to them. Why would they help me?"

Mark takes his father's hand, narrowing his gaze.

"Because that's what I taught them."

# Priceless Day

Mr. Baker's phone rings nonstop. Whether it's business meetings, deadlines, or his overbearing boss, he never has a moment to himself. Stress and worries fill his days.

"I never have enough time," he blasts.

One day, his elderly neighbour, Mr. Chen, notices him looking down. "Hey, are you okay?" he shouts from his garden.

"Not really; I've got so much to do but not enough time to do it," Mr. Baker replies.

"Well, I have a challenge for you," Mr. Chen says. "It might help you see things clearer."

Mr. Baker leans in closer. "A challenge?"

Mr. Chen nods. "Spend one whole day doing only free activities. If you succeed, I'll reveal the secret to a good and fulfilling life."

Mr. Baker laughs the request off. "I've got no time for that. I'm way too busy. But thanks anyway."

But over the next few days, work and stress begin to take their toll on Mr. Baker once more.

His health begins to degrade rapidly. He must do something drastic.

That's when he remembers the old man's challenge. With nothing to lose, he decides to do it.

He immediately turns his phone off and puts his laptop away, setting off for a day without schedules or deadlines.

Mr. Baker decides to first take a walk through the park. He listens to the bird's chirp, watches the squirrels, and even feeds the ducks.

He begins to feel lighter, finding himself smiling for the first time in years.

Suddenly, he spots an old friend that he hasn't seen in years.

He approaches him, and they spend the next couple of hours catching up, reminiscing, and laughing about the old days.

As afternoon approaches, he says his goodbyes to his friend, promising to meet up again.

He then decides to wander into the public library, soon finding himself lost in the books he had always promised to read.

As evening approaches, Mr. Baker decides to walk home. On his way, he notices a sign: "Volunteers are needed at the City Youth Shelter."

He decides to check it out. Upon his arrival, he immediately begins helping others - serving meals, cleaning the floor, and playing with the younger children.

He feels a sense of purpose he has never felt before.

He rushes to Mr. Chen's house to find out the secret he had promised him.

He finds Mr. Chen in the garden.

"I did it!" Mr. Baker exclaims. "I spent the whole day doing free activities. So, now you need to tell me - what's the secret to a good and fulfilling life?"

Mr. Chen looks up, smiling.

"You've already found it, Mr. Baker.

# A Mother's Sacrifice

Maria loves her daughter Lily more than life itself, prepared to do anything for her.

Lily loves to play the piano, and she has talent too. But lessons are expensive.

Maria decides to work extra hours to pay for them. As each day passes, Lily gets better and better.

Her music teacher advises her to apply for the prestigious Harmony Youth Academy, a specialized school for gifted musicians.

Lily applies and is soon accepted, but there's a problem: the fees are huge. Determined to give her daughter the best life possible, Maria takes on another job and even skips meals to raise the funds.

Eventually, they have enough, and Lily attends the school.

Lily excels, becoming better every day.

Years pass, and her time at the academy is a success. But there is one last hurdle: university.

The fees are high, and Maria is already working multiple jobs. She can't skip any more meals.

All hope seems lost.

One day, Maria walks past a jewellery shop with a sign that reads, "We buy anything." Without a moment's hesitation, she sells her prized ring. The amount is exactly what they need.

Lily notices her mom's bare finger. "Mom, where's your ring? Did you lose it?"

Maria smiles. "I found something more valuable."

Lily goes on to achieve success, graduating from university and immediately being signed to a record label.

She sells countless records and is selected to perform at the world's premier music theatre.

Her performance is outstanding.

After the performance, amid a storm of applause, Lily rushes to her mother. "Mom, I know how hard you worked to allow me to be the person I am today. So I have a gift for you."

She hands her mother a small velvet box. Maria opens it to find an exact replica of her old wedding ring.

"Sorry, it's not the real one, but it's as close as I could get," Lily states.

"It's amazing," Maria replies, shocked. "But how did you know what it looked like?"

Lily smiles.

"Well, years ago, I figured you sold your favourite ring to allow me to achieve my dreams. I knew I wouldn't be able to get the exact ring back, so I've been drawing it ever since. I always knew I'd replace it someday."

# The Hero in the Hallway

Ms. Johnson's 5th-grade class buzzes with excitement. Today is a special assignment day.

"I have an important task for you all," Ms. Johnson states. She writes on the board in big letters: "WHO IS YOUR HERO?"

"I want you to write about someone you consider a hero," Ms. Johnson explains. "Think carefully. Heroes come in all shapes and sizes."

Excitement fills the room.

"I'm writing about LeBron James!"

"I'm choosing Taylor Swift!"

"I'm definitely choosing Messi!"

In the back of the class, little Tim chews his pencil thoughtfully. He already knows who his hero is.

The next week, the students work hard on their essays.

Tim spends hours perfecting his, even staying behind after school to finish it.

Presentation day soon arrives. One by one, students stand up to talk about famous athletes, singers, and movie stars.

Then it's Tim's turn.

His hands shake as he walks to the front of the class, but his voice is steady. "My hero is Mr. Garcia, our school janitor," he begins.

The class bursts out laughing.

"A janitor? They are complete losers!"

"What's wrong with you?"

"Choose a real hero!" his classmate's shout.

But Tim stays strong. He takes a deep breath and continues.

"Mr. Garcia is always smiling. He helps people no matter what. He stays late to clean up after school events without extra pay. Not only this, but he uses his own money to buy supplies for students who can't afford them."

As Tim speaks, the atmosphere in the classroom changes.

Students begin to take notice.

When Tim finishes, the room is silent.

Ms. Johnson moves to the front of the class. "Now, I have a surprise for you all," she announces. "As you all know, we've been looking for our next class president. This person needs to be kind, honest, and selfless."

The students wait in anticipation.

"I asked a special person to choose—the owner of the school."

Everyone's face drops as the owner walks in.

It's Mr. Garcia.

"Hello, everyone," Mr. Garcia says warmly. "Ms. Johnson asked me to choose your next class president. It is an easy choice.

I chose the only student who noticed me: Tim."

# The Most Precious Gift

Mr. Davis prides himself on his generosity. Every month, he donates huge amounts of money to various charities, feeling that he has done his good deed for the month.

On Monday morning, Mr. Davis's boss makes an announcement. "Our company is starting a new initiative; every employee must volunteer for one day at Sunny Grove Shelter."

Mr. Davis frowns. He has important work to do.

"Why waste time when I could just give them money?" he asks.

"It's the rules, Mr. Davis," his boss replies firmly.

The day of volunteering soon arrives, and Mr. Davis drags himself to Sunny Grove, planning to do the bare minimum and leave as soon as possible.

A cheerful coordinator greets him. "You'll be reading to our elderly residents today," she says, handing him a stack of books.

Mr. Davis sighs, thinking to himself, "This is going to be a long day."

He settles into a chair in the common room, his eyes glued to the clock.

An elderly woman in a floral dress sits nearby. "Hello," she says softly. "I'm Mrs. Steveston. What will you be reading today?"

Mr. Davis picks up the first book, barely glancing at the title. "This one," he states unenthusiastically.

As he begins to read, his voice flat and uninterested, he notices Mrs. Steveston becoming a little emotional. Halfway through the first chapter, Mr. Davis hears a sniffle. He looks up to see tears rolling down Mrs. Steveston's cheeks.

Alarmed, he asks, "Mrs. Steveston, are you okay?"

She dabs at her eyes with a tissue. "I'm fine, dear. It's just that no one has read to me since my Harold passed away. I'd forgotten how wonderful it feels."

Mr. Davis feels a lump in his throat. He looks at Mrs. Steveston and sees the loneliness in her eyes, the tremor in her hands as she clutches the tissue. At that moment, something shifts inside him.

The clock forgotten, Mr. Davis clears his throat and begins reading again, this time with warmth and dedication. Hours pass, and he ends up reading all sorts of books.

As the day ends, Mr. Davis realizes he has stayed far longer than required, but strangely, he doesn't mind at all.

As he is about to leave, Mrs. Steveston grasps his hand. "Thank you for today, Mr. Davis. You've given me such a precious gift."

Puzzled, Mr. Davis asks, "Really? What gift was that?"

Mrs. Steveston's eyes widen.

"Your time."

# Epiphany

"Get off my sidewalk!" Mr. Granger shouts.

"We are only playing," the kids reply innocently.

"I don't care. Leave," he growls.

Mr. Granger is an angry man.

He especially hates kids playing outside his house.

Everyone in the neighbourhood calls him Mr. Miserable.

One sunny day, he hears a commotion outside, followed
by a sudden knock at the door.

He opens it to find a sweet little girl, no older than 8
years old, standing in front.

"Hey, sorry, sir, we accidentally kicked our ball into your
garden. Could you get it for us?" she whispers

Mr. Grange's fists shake with rage, but he has a cunning
thought. He decides to get the ball, not as a good deed,
but to puncture it right in front of the children, to teach
them a lesson and set an example.

"Yes, of course, dear. No problem," he replies, smirking.

Mr. Granger enters his garden but can't see the ball.
Then, from the corner of his eye, he spots it.

It's inside his shed.

As he enters, he notices it has knocked a picture on the floor, the frame is smashed but the photo inside is still intact.

His face turns red with anger. "Wasting my time and breaking my property. I can't wait to show them justice," he mutters to himself.

He bends down to retrieve the faded photograph from the ground.

Curious about what it is, he turns it over and gasps what he sees: a photo of him when he was younger, playing soccer in the park with all his old friends.

Great memories flood his brain, and he finds himself smiling. He places the photograph in his pocket, retrieves the ball, and proceeds to the front door.

The girl's eyes light up as she sees the ball in his hands. "Thank you so much!" she shouts bouncing from toe to toe.

"Before I give it to you, I wanted to ask you a question," Mr. Granger says.

The girl frowns. "Erm, okay'

"Can I play with you guys?" he inquires.

The girl blinks rapidly. "Of course you can. It's fun to have a grownup play with us." She remarks.

Mr. Granger begins to play with the kids.

Soon, more and more children arrive. "Can we play too?" they ask.

"Of course. The more, the merrier," Mr. Granger insists.

They play all day long until sunset. After the children leave, Mr. Granger makes his way back to his house but is suddenly approached by his neighbour.

"Hi, sorry, I hope you don't mind, but I've never seen you that happy or nice to the children. What changed?" the neighbour asks.

Mr. Granger smiles and looks down at the worn photo in his hand.

"Oh, not much. I just remembered who I used to be."

# The Sweetest Gesture

The bell above the door jingles as Tommy walks into Sweety's Bakery. The smell of fresh doughnuts makes his mouth water.

Armed with a single dollar bill crinkled in his pocket, his entire week's allowance, he enters the donut store.

Behind the counter, Ms. Jen, the waitress, looks stressed with her head in her hands. Tommy approaches the counter.

"Excuse me," he says politely. "How much for two doughnuts, please?"

Ms. Jen barely acknowledges him. "One dollar," she replies.

Tommy thinks for a second. "Okay, and so how much for just one doughnut?"

Ms. Jen slams her fists on the counter. "Are you kidding me?" she snaps. "Two doughnuts are a dollar. One doughnut is fifty cents. It's simple math!"

"I'm sorry," Tommy whimpers.

"Look, I'm having a really bad day. Just tell me what you want!" the waitress growls.

He smiles. "I'll just take the one doughnut then, please."

She thrusts a fresh chocolate-glazed doughnut into his hands and carries on with her day.

Tommy sits at a small table, savouring every bite of his treat.

He watches Ms. Jen rush around tirelessly, serving customers and clearing tables.

When he finishes, he stands up to leave. But before he does, he pulls something from his pocket and leaves it on the table.

Later, as the bakery quiets down, Ms. Jen approaches Tommy's table to clean it.

But guilt washes over her as she sees what he's left behind.

There, next to a neatly folded napkin, sit two shiny quarters.

Beside them is a small note scribbled in childish handwriting:

"Sorry I annoyed you. I hope this can brighten your day. - Tommy"

# The Wish Maker

Every night for years at 11:11, Sarah closes her eyes and makes a wish, hoping magic can change her life.

But each morning, she wakes up to the same old routine. Nothing ever changes.

On her 30th birthday, Sarah stares at the clock as it turns to 11:11. She opens her mouth to make a wish, then stops.

"Enough," she says aloud, her voice firm. "It's time to make my own magic."

The next day, Sarah grabs a notebook and writes down her three biggest wishes: find a purpose, have an adventure, and achieve success.

She looks at the list, determined to make it happen.

The following day, while walking to work, she spots a vacancy for a volunteer at an animal shelter.

She signs up immediately, spending every Saturday helping and feeling a sense of joy she's never experienced before.

A few months later, she sees an ad on her computer for a trip to a place she hasn't even heard of - Cambodia.

Without a moment's hesitation, she books it. Within days, she boards the plane and sets off to explore lands unknown, all by herself.

She arrives back a few weeks later, rejuvenated. On her trip, she had an idea to start a travel recommendation website.

She gets started right away, learning web design, sales, and marketing, working tirelessly day and night to build her business.

Weeks turn into months, and months into years. Then, one starry night, Sarah glances at her clock by chance. The number 11:11 glows back at her.

She's shocked, realizing she hasn't made a wish in years.

Suddenly, as she ponders this, her phone rings.

"Hello, Sarah?" It's Mark from the animal shelter. "I'm calling to thank you for five years of dedicated service. Just wanted to let you know we're naming our new cat playroom after you!"

Stunned, Sarah hangs up and decides to check her laptop.

A notification pops up - her travel blog has just hit one million subscribers.

Then, her email pings. It's from a major business magazine, requesting an interview about her successful web design company.

Sarah leans back in her chair wearing huge smile. She has everything she wanted, yet she hasn't made a wish in years.

As the clock turns to 11:12, it clicks, she finally understands.

"The magic was never in the wishing," she whispers.

"It was in the doing all along."

# The Weight of Words

"You're so slow, Tommy! What a loser!" Jake hisses.

"Shut up, Jake! You're such a jerk!" Tommy retorts.

Scoutmaster Dan frowns. He had hoped this trip would bring the boys together, not drive them apart. It is time for a lesson.

"Alright, gang! Gather round," Scoutmaster Dan calls out. The boys huddle close.

"I have a new rule," he announces. "Every time you say something unkind, you must pick up a rock and put it in your backpack. No exceptions."

The boys raise an eyebrow, giving one another a confused look, but everyone agrees.

As the day wears on, backpacks grow heavier and heavier.

One boy, Jake, finds his bag particularly full.

By the time they reach the campsite, exhaustion has set in. Their faces are red, shoulders slumped, and feet tired. They all lie exhausted on the ground.

Jake, a particularly troublesome boy, approaches Scoutmaster Dan, his backpack bulging.

"Sir, I can't do this anymore. It's too heavy," he states, depleted.

Scoutmaster Dan looks at the tired faces around him.

"Alright, scouts. Here's a new rule," he says. "For every kind thing you say or do, you can remove one rock from your pack."

At first, the kindness feels forced, used selfishly to rid themselves of rocks. But soon, genuine smiles begin to appear.

"Here, Tommy, let me help you with your tent."

"Great job on the fire, Jake!"

"Docs anyone want to share my cookies?"

One by one, rocks are removed. Backpacks lighten. Spirits grow.

As the sun begins to set, Jake approaches Scoutmaster Dan again. This time, he is grinning, his backpack empty. "Sir, it feels so much better without all that extra weight."

Scoutmaster Dan smiles.

That same night, the troops gather around the campfire. Scoutmaster Dan stands up.

"Scouts, today you learned an important lesson. Hate and anger are like rocks in your backpack. They weigh you down and make the journey harder. But kindness? That sets you free."

# A Dropped Wallet

Mr. Gold's polished shoes click against the cracked sidewalk of Elm Street. Every day, like clockwork, he visits the same poor neighbourhood.

His tailored suit is a stark contrast to the worn buildings around him. The locals watch him curiously, wondering why such a wealthy man visits their part of town so often.

As Mr. Gold reaches the corner of the street, he reaches into his pocket.

A sleek leather wallet, bulging with cash, slips from his hand and falls to the ground.

Suddenly, a figure darts from the shadows, snatches the wallet, and disappears down an alley.

Mr. Gold sighs and continues his walk.

Day after day, Mr. Gold repeats this routine, dropping a brand-new wallet every day. Each time, a different person takes the wallet.

He watches them go, his eyes a mix of hope and disappointment.

The neighbourhood buzzes with rumours. Some think Mr. Gold is crazy, while others believe he is playing a cruel game.

One crisp autumn morning, Mr. Gold's wallet slips from his fingers as usual, but this time, something different happens.

"Hey, mister!" a voice calls out. "You dropped your wallet!"

Mr. Gold turns to see a homeless man in tattered clothes hurrying towards him, wallet in hand.

"Here you go, sir," the man says, handing him the wallet. "Thank you so much. You know, you should be more careful around here. This is a struggling area. Not everyone is like me."

"Oh, I won't worry," Mr. Gold replies with a smile.

"Sir, before you leave, I have a question that's been puzzling me," the homeless man inquires.

"Okay, go ahead," Mr. Gold encourages him.

"Well, I've seen you drop your wallet here almost every day for months. Why do you keep coming back every day doing the same thing? Are you okay?"

"Oh yes, I'm more than okay," Mr. Gold assures him.

"So why do it?" the homeless man asks, his brow furrowed in confusion.

Mr. Gold's smile widens. "Oh, I'm looking to change somebody's life."

The homeless man looks even more perplexed. "Well, why haven't you? You've had plenty of chances."

Mr. Gold places a hand on the homeless man's shoulder, his eyes wide.

"I was waiting for somebody like you."

# Weird Girl

Sarah always sits alone at lunch. Her classmates avoid her, their whispers filling the air around her table.

"She never talks to anyone," one says.

"I heard she hasn't spoken since kindergarten," another adds.

"What a weirdo," a third chimes in.

One day, a new boy named Michael joins the class. As lunchtime comes, he scans the cafeteria and notices Sarah sitting alone.

Without hesitation, he heads towards her table.

"Hey, new kid!" a classmate calls out. "Don't sit there. That's where the weirdo sits."

"Yeah, she never talks to anyone," another warns.

Michael pauses, looking from his classmates to Sarah. With a small shake of his head, he continues and sits across from her.

Sarah's eyes widen in surprise, but she says nothing.

Every day that week, Michael sits with Sarah.

On Friday, he brings two cupcakes to lunch.

"I thought we could use a treat," he says, placing one in front of Sarah and making sure to face her directly. "My mom made these. They're really good!"

Sarah stares at the cupcake, then slowly raises her eyes to meet Michael's. Her lip's part, and in a soft, uncertain voice, she says, "Thank you."

Michael's jaw drops. "You can talk!" he exclaims, a grin spreading across his face.

Sarah nods. "Of course I can," she replies, her voice growing stronger. "But I'm deaf. I've been hoping for someone to face me so I could read their lips. You're the first person who has."

# The Invisible Wish

Staring in the mirror, Sarah wonders when her life is going to get better.

She does the same thing every day, always finding something new to complain about, whether it's at work, home life, or friendships. Nothing is ever good enough.

"If only I could be truly happy," she says. "If only I could make a real difference in the world."

One rainy Saturday, as Sarah rummages through her dusty attic, her hand brushes against something smooth and cold. She pulls out an old, tarnished lamp.

"Probably just more junk," Sarah grumbles. As she rubs it to clean off the dust, a puff of glittering smoke erupts from the spout.

A genie suddenly materializes before her.

"Greetings!" he shouts. "I'll grant you one wish. Choose wisely!"

Sarah's heart races. This is her chance! "I wish to be happy," she blurts out, "to make a difference in the world!"

The genie's eyes twinkle. He snaps his fingers, and in a blink, he is gone.

Sarah goes to bed, hoping for a better day, but her days stay the same. Nothing changes. Her job is still the same, her bank account hasn't increased, and the world outside her window hasn't transformed.

She becomes annoyed. Anger begins to bubble up inside her.

After a few days of nothingness, she decides to confront the genie once more. She runs to the attic, grabs the lamp, and rubs it immediately.

The genie reappears, still smiling. "You tricked me!" Sarah accuses. "Nothing's different!"

"Look closer," he whispers. "Let me show you."

With a wave of his hand, the genie conjures misty visions in the air.

Sarah sees herself from the day before, holding the elevator for a coworker rushing to make it in time for an important meeting, sharing half her sandwich with a stray dog in the park, and pausing on her walk home to admire a brilliant sunset.

"But... but those are just little things," Sarah whispers, her anger fading to confusion.

The genie nods. "Exactly. Happiness isn't a destination, Sarah. It's not something big that happens to you. It's in the little moments, the small kindnesses, the beauty we choose to see."

# Richest Boy on the Block

Two houses stand side by side.

One is a grand mansion with manicured lawns and shiny windows.

The other is a small, cozy cottage with a vegetable garden and a tire swing.

Every day, Tommy from the mansion leans over the fence to talk to Joey from the cottage.

"Hey, Joey," Tommy calls out. "Look at our house! It's huge! It's way bigger than yours."

Joey smiles but says nothing.

"Check out our brand-new lighting system," Tommy continues. "People can see our house from miles away. Look at all the toys I get to play with every day. Bet you wish you could have them."

Again, Joey simply smiles back.

The pattern continues for weeks, with Tommy boasting about his family's latest luxuries and Joey always responding with a gentle smile.

One day, Joey and his dad are sitting on their porch swing.

His father decides to ask him a question. "Son, doesn't it upset you when Tommy brags like that every day?"

Joey looks up at his dad. "Nope. It makes me feel better."

His father frowns. "Better? But how?"

"Well, he's right. His house is bigger than ours," Joey explains. "But I like our small house. It means I can find you faster if I have a problem."

"He may brag about the bright lights, but we have all the lights we need in the night sky above. Sure, Tommy has many toys, but he plays alone. His dad often works away. He's never there to play with him like you are."

Joey pauses, a thoughtful smile on his face. "You know, Dad, I like it when Tommy says those things."

"Why's that, son?" his dad asks softly.

"Because every time he does, he reminds me of just how rich I am,"

# The Bike Jump

Jack and Ryan are two best friends who do everything together, never leaving one another's side.

One day, Jack gets a new bike and suddenly becomes the most popular boy in school. Everyone wants to look at his bike.

A group of older boys approaches Jack and asks if he wants to try his new bike out on the ramps nearby.

Excited by the attention from the older kids who have never wanted to play with him before, Jack agrees.

Ryan tries to talk him out of it, warning, "Those ramps are dangerous, Jack."

But Jack doesn't care. "Leave me alone," he shouts. "I've got new friends now!"

He sets off for the ramps.

When he arrives, Jack is shocked to see that the ramps are much bigger than he had thought. He hesitates, saying, "I think they are a little too big for me, actually, guys."

But the older kids pressure him. "Come on, don't be a baby! You can't chicken out now," they shout.

Feeling like he has no choice, Jack approaches the ramp at high speed. His bike flies through the air, but he's unable to land it. He falls hard, seriously injuring himself.

The older kids panic and flee the scene, leaving Jack all alone.

A stranger sees the boy on the ground and calls an ambulance.

At the hospital, doctors tell Jack that he was very lucky and could have lost his leg.

While relieved, Jack feels sad that he has lost all of his new "friends."

As he sits alone in an empty hospital room, Jack hears footsteps. The door bursts open, and there stands his old friend, Ryan.

Jack's eyes light up. "Ryan, you came?" he exclaims.

Ryan smiles warmly.

"Of course I did. I'm your best friend, remember?"

# Bully

Timmy, a little boy, is always in trouble at school. His parents come to bail him out and defend him no matter what.

One day, Timmy smashes a school window. His parents come right away and pay for the damages.

Later, he paints graffiti on a wall. Again, his parents rush to the boy's defence.

"Oh, principal, he didn't mean to do any harm," they say. "It's just part of growing up."

The next day, Timmy gets in trouble for bullying another student.

The principal calls his parents, and the boy waits for them to come and help him. But they don't arrive.

Timmy waits in the cold for hours after school. Other kids point and laugh at him, shouting, "Where are your parents now?"

Hours pass, and eventually, his parents arrive to pick him up.

"Where have you been?!" Timmy screams. "Why didn't you come to help me sooner?!"

His parents narrow their gaze towards him, their expressions serious.

"How did it feel to be left here and laughed at?" they ask.

"It was horrible," Timmy admits. "I still can't believe you did that to me."

"We know," his parents reply.

"Now you know how it feels to be like the other children you bullied."

# Money

Karl, a wealthy man, spends every weekend throwing lavish and wild parties that often get out of hand.

He acts recklessly, not caring for other people's safety or well-being.

One night, he throws a huge party. Karl dances around, constantly bumping into people. He spills his drink all over a guest's dress, leaving them furious.

"Oh, who cares? It's just a dress. Buy a new one," he shouts, throwing money at their feet.

Karl then lets off a firework, damaging the house next door.

The neighbours are infuriated and demand an immediate apology.

"It's just a house. Get it repaired," Karl states, throwing money at them once more. "That should cover it!"

Later that evening, he accidentally knocks a statue off the balcony, damaging a couple of cars below. Enraged, the car owners approach him.

"What have you done to our car?" they bark.

"It's just a few scratches. Anyway, who cares? Just get it fixed," Karl remarks, throwing money at them.

Soon the party is over, and Karl passes out on the sofa.

The next morning, he decides to take his dog for a walk but can't find him anywhere. He searches everywhere, calling the dog's name, but there's no response.

From the corner of his eye, Karl notices something poking out from the rubble of the statue he knocked over. It's his dog.

Panicking, he picks up the dog and rushes to the vet immediately.

Karl bursts through the doors, screaming, "Please help my dog. I don't care what it costs. I have all the money in the world! Just save him."

He throws money on the desk.

The vet looks down at the dog, then back up at Karl.

"I'm so sorry, sir. I'm afraid it's too late."

The vet's expression is sombre as he continues, "You can have all the money in the world. It can buy a lot of things, but it can't buy life."

# Gold

A billionaire, who used to be homeless, feels inspired to visit a shelter that he was once a part of.

He brings with him a solid gold brick and stands before a crowd.

"Put your hand up if you want the gold," he calls out.

Everyone's hands shoot up.

He then pulls out a hammer and beats the gold with it.

\"Who wants it now?" he asks.

Once more, everyone's hands fly up.

Next, he takes out a knife and carves into the gold violently, scratching it all over.

"Who wants it now?" he questions.

Still, everyone's hands stay up.

The billionaire proceeds to jump on the gold, kicking it across the floor.'

"Who wants it now?"

Yet again, everyone's hands remain raised.

He pauses, holding the gold up to the crowd.

"This gold was beaten, stabbed, kicked, and trampled on," he says solemnly. "Yet you still wanted it. Why?"

The crowd falls silent, hanging on his every word.

"Because its value never changed," the billionaire explains.

"No matter what happens, always remember: you are the gold."

# Thanks for reading.

If you liked the stories, then check out the second book in the collection.

Just click the link below:

https://mybook.to/InspiringStories2

Or scan the QR code below:

Until next time,

Christopher Starr

Made in the USA
Monee, IL
21 March 2025

14383059R00052